THE
CATCH

F
Travel
C

THE
CATCH

Rick *Jasper*

MINNEAPOLIS

Darby Creek
A division of Lerner Publishing Group, Inc.
241 First Avenue North
Minneapolis, MN 55401 U.S.A.

Website address: www.lernerbooks.com

The images in this book are used with the permission of:
© Kelpfish/Dreamstime.com, p. 109; © iStockphoto.com/Jill Fromer, p. 112 (banner background); © iStockphoto.com/Naphtalina, pp. 112, 113, 114 (brickwall background). Front Cover: © Stephen Mcsweeny /Shutterstock Images, (blue sky), © Alfo/Alloy/CORBIS (baseball player). Back Cover: © Kelpfish/Dreamstime.com.

Jasper, Rick, 1948–
    The catch / by Rick Jasper.
        p.   cm. — (Travel team)
    ISBN 978–0–7613–8320–8 (lib. bdg. : alk. paper)
        [1. Baseball—Fiction.] I. Title.
    PZ7.J32Cat 2012
    [Fic]—dc23   2011024899

Manufactured in the United States of America
1 – BP – 12/31/11

*To my grandmother,
Anna Reece, who actually saw
Babe Ruth play*

"The way a team plays as a whole determines its success. You may have the greatest bunch of individual stars in the world, but if they don't play together, the club won't be worth a dime."

—BABE RUTH

CHAPTER 1

*I*t all began with The Catch. If you say that, "The Catch," to anyone who was playing for the Las Vegas Roadrunners that day, they still know what you mean. And you can still watch it on YouTube and other websites. It will probably live online, somewhere, forever.

It happened a year ago in the quarter finals of the Palm Springs Invitational Tournament. For U17 traveling teams, the Palm is a big deal. It comes at the end of the season, and the best teams from west of the Rockies are there. Not to mention a ton of college and pro scouts and TV cameras.

The Runners were the designated home team in that game, and they were a run up on the Phoenix Desert Eagles in the bottom of the ninth. There was one out and an Eagle on first: Jimmy Toms, one of their speedsters. Unfortunately for Eagles fans, their number-nine hitter was at the plate. That was little Kenny Bailey. He was a terrific infielder, but he had already struck out three times in the game. The outfielders were playing shallow.

Maybe Kenny was frustrated, or desperate. With a 1–2 count, he should have known they were sending Jimmy to second and just tried to hit something sharp behind the runner. Instead, he practically left his feet swinging at a fastball.

There was a sharp *clowp!* as Kenny connected and sent a rising line drive lasering for the fence in deep right center. You can hear the commentary on YouTube:

"And there it goes! Toms is off, this will definitely tie the game! Hold it, look

*at the center fielder! Danny Manuel is
flying after that drive. There's no way
he can catch up . . . but he's gaining, he's
gaining . . . He dives flat out and . . . Oh.
My. Gosh! He's caught it. He throws from
the ground to second, who throws to first
and they've doubled up Toms. Game over!
Do you believe that? Let's watch it again."*

And they did. Again and again. In Vegas
the TV news shows were actually leading
with the clip—a sports story beating out the
murders and car wrecks. When the video
made ESPN, the analysts had a few more
words:

*"How did that kid catch up with that? He
must be psychic!"*

*"I know, Boomer. It almost looked like
he was after that ball before it left the bat."*

The video footage is amazing to watch.
The pitcher winds up, the runner goes, Kenny
swings for the fences and . . . The rest seems
almost like slow motion, even when it isn't.

The fielder is racing after the ball, and then at some point the ball is trying to outrun the fielder. And just when it seems a catch is impossible, Manuel goes airborne and horizontal. Like the dude should have been wearing a cape.

Suddenly Manuel has the ball. He lands on the ground in a heap, but he holds on and raises the ball to show he's made the catch. Toms, the base runner, has just rounded third when he stops, looks back at the third-base coach yelling and waving his arms, and reverses his field. But he knows it's hopeless. Manuel suddenly looks at Perez, who's also yelling, and throws him the ball. Perez throws to first. The crowd goes nuts. Manuel trots in, and when he gets to the infield his teammates swarm over him, finally hoisting him on their shoulders and carrying him to the dugout.

Quite a catch. Quite a play. I can hardly believe it was me.

CHAPTER 2

*I*n the dugout, everyone was hollering and slapping me on the back except the coaches. Coach Harris was writing something in his notebook. Coach Washington, his assistant, finally came over and put a hand on my shoulder. Then he took me to one side.

"Congratulations, Danny," he said. "Great catch." There was something else in his eyes, though. "You know," he said next, "it was the wrong play."

"What do ya mean, Wash?" I got defensive. "We won!"

"We did, Danny. But what do you think were the odds of you making that catch?"

"One in a million," I grinned. "That's why it was . . ."

"That's why it was the wrong play. If you miss, we lose. Bailey had the speed to take all four bases if it got by you. If you play the ball off the fence, we're tied with Bailey on second. You've got a good arm—maybe we even have a shot at nailing him there."

"But, Wash . . ."—Why couldn't he see this?—"We won!"

"Yeah. We won the lottery."

Whatever. I wasn't about to let Wash bring me down with all that. I was enjoying the moment. Next thing I knew there was a hot girl in a T-shirt that said PEPPERDINE, the Malibu university, across the front, putting a microphone in my face.

"Danny," she said, "that was incredible. What was going through your mind when that ball was hit?"

"Just, you know, get it," I said.

"How did you have the presence of mind to start the double play?"

The truth is that credit belonged to Sammy. All I was thinking at the time was, *I made the catch.* But I didn't tell her that. "Well, we're always coached to keep the situation in mind," I said, noticing Wash watching from the other end of the dugout.

"Have you thought yet about your baseball future?"

"Nah. I'm just thinking about tomorrow's game." Another lie. At the moment, I was thinking about PEPPERDINE and also about when I could see video of the catch. And about my dad. I hoped he'd seen the play, and I couldn't wait to hear his reaction.

. . .

After we all dressed up the team went to dinner. The Palm is a first-class tournament. The team roomed at a spa, and they always had a huge spread waiting for us at mealtime.

I should have felt great, but Wash had spoiled it. I kept chewing on what he had said.

I filled my plate and looked for Nellie.

Nelson "Nellie" Carville is our third baseman. He's more than that, though. Some guys just have the "leader" thing going on, and Nellie's the guy who has it on our team. That's why he's captain.

There was a space next to him at one of the tables, so I sat down there.

"Hey Danny," he said. "Mad catch!"

"Thanks," I said. "I'm glad you said that." Then I told him about Wash.

Nellie listened till I was through, and then he thought a minute. "Don't let it bring you down," he said finally. "It was a beautiful thing to see. Now, Wash's job is to teach us how to play better. Nobody can teach a catch like you made. But Coach was trying to teach you something, right?"

"Yeah, I guess he was saying, 'Think about the situation.'"

"Yep. So next time . . . But tonight, enjoy the moment. The team sure is."

I felt better. Nellie has that effect on people.

A minute later my phone buzzed. It was Dad's number, but when I said, "Yo," the voice I heard was Sal's. Sal is my dad's "associate." That's how my dad always introduces him. "This is Sal Ruberto, my associate." He and my dad have been working together since I was little. I've never been sure exactly what they do, but as dad always says, it puts meat on the table.

"Hey Danny," Sal said, "You're famous! Your dad's watching that catch on TV. Here, he wants to talk to you."

CHAPTER *3*

"Danny!" I could tell Dad was in a great mood, and I felt as good as I'd felt all day. "Wow, what a play! I must have watched it a dozen times, fast-mo, slow-mo. It's a thing of beauty, son."

I could hear a phone ringing in the background. "Thanks, Dad!"

Dad asked me to hold a second. He said something to Sal, and then he came back on. "Sorry, Danny, my phone's been ringing ever since your video came on the news. Ringing with opportunities!"

"Yeah? Like what?"

"We'll talk about all that when you get home, Dan. Right now you just need to focus on baseball. You're in the semis tomorrow. Tough team?"

"Same team. We're both one and one. But we're facing their best pitcher. I hear he could be tournament MVP."

"Well, you go get 'em. Hey, I need to ask a favor."

"Sure."

"There'll be a guy at the game tomorrow. Name is Strauss, Jack Strauss. He's a business friend, and he was real excited about your play. He wants to meet you."

"No problem."

"Great, great. Okay, you rest up tonight. I'll talk to you after the game tomorrow."

After the call, I wondered if this guy was some kind of scout, or maybe just a fan. Dad had called him a "business friend." But that didn't mean much because I had a pretty sketchy idea of what Dad's business even was. My older sister, Melina—we call her Mel— would joke about it sometimes. Every time we tried to pin Dad down about what he did, we got a different story: "Oh, it's not interesting, just business." Or "Buying and selling. You know, investments." Or the colorful version: "I guess you could say I'm a gambler."

Our mom died from cancer when we were both in grade school, and we'd had what Dad called "governesses" ever since to take care of stuff at home. A lot of times, before we had licenses, Sal would drive us to school and practices, and sometimes his concern for our well-being was almost motherly. In fact, behind his back Mel called him Aunt Sally, which was especially funny if you saw him—six feet four inches, 250 pounds, and very hairy. So we weren't on our own, and Dad was home a lot, unless he had a business trip; his main office was in our house. He worked hard. And while we never felt rich, we always had whatever we needed.

. . .

After supper, some of the guys who had family with them went out to movies or shopping. I went to my room, which I was sharing this trip with Shotaro Mori, one of our pitchers, usually in relief. As a roommate, Shotaro was low maintenance. He was—during the Palm—having a passionate affair with his Xbox. So he was gaming, and I was just chilling in the room when Mel called.

"Hey, little brother, you got me in trouble!"

"What do ya mean?"

"One of the girls here has a kid brother on the Eagles. And you definitely rained on her parade." Then she laughed. Mel's laugh is special. "So," she went on, "where did you find that catch?"

"I don't really know. I saw it was gonna be hit, and I just took off running."

Mel is the best athlete in our family. Since girls don't get to go very far in baseball, she got into softball when she was twelve. Today she's playing shortstop for Arizona State University, which is one of the best women's softball teams in the country. There's talk of her being an All-American. Mel's been on TV a lot more than me.

Then I told her what Wash had said. I just couldn't seem to let that go.

She listened and then said, "Yeah, that's what coaches are for, keeping your head small. Our coach is always telling us to think past the play. But you were spectacular."

"Thanks, sis. Coming from you that means a lot. Well, we've got the Eagles again tomorrow. Hope I can get you in some more trouble with your friend. Whichever one of us wins goes to the finals."

"Wish I could watch. They haven't offered you a TV contract yet?"

"Not yet."

"Okay. I'll call tomorrow night if I can. Good luck, bro!"

That night as I went to sleep I was thinking about the Eagles, trying to remember anything that would help me the next day. What the next day would actually bring, though, I could never have imagined.

CHAPTER 4

The game was scheduled for 10:00 A.M. They tried not to have games in the heat and wind of the early afternoon in the desert, and they were saving the evening for the first game of the finals. With luck, we'd be playing twice that day.

On the bus to the field Coach Harris had a few words for us. I'd seen Coach look better, but he always seemed to wear the tension on his face before a big game. He'd probably been up all night trying to figure out ways for us to win.

"Okay, men," he started. "You've seen this team before. Every guy is fast. They play small ball better than anyone else you'll face. And they're pitching Scott today."

The team was quiet. He meant Troy Scott, a skinny, six-foot-five-inch kid who could bring a ninety-mile-per-hour fastball. Which set up his other pitch—a changeup. Not much of a curve, but he didn't need one. Our hitters would be guessing between fast and slow.

"Wash and I were looking at film last night," Harris went on. "What did we see, Wash?"

Wash stood up. "Sometimes," he said, "not always, Troy tips his change. Watch his glove. Sometimes he'll squeeze it around his pitching hand, like this, before he starts his windup."

Harris resumed. "Infielders, be on your toes. These hitters know how to work the ball. Outfielders, play smart. You know *they* will. Pay attention to their base runners. Know the situation. Know the score."

We got to the field at nine o'clock and started warming up. The Eagles arrived not long after us. And there were a lot of fans for a morning game. Usually we had a few team family members, but today there were quite a few people I didn't recognize. The Catch had probably gotten some folks interested.

One guy sitting in the front row behind our dugout stood out. He was fat and red-faced, fifty or so years old. He wore a white suit, a blue-and-white-striped dress shirt, a red tie, and a white, broad-brimmed hat. Even though it was early, the day was hot—we were in the desert after all—and this guy's suit was already a mass of wrinkles. He had a white handkerchief the size of a towel, and every so often he'd take off the hat and wipe the sweat from his shaved head. He looked uncomfortable in the midst of all the shorts and T-shirts in the stands.

There was one other person I noticed, sitting up a few rows behind the plate in an orange halter-top. When she saw me look up that way she waved. You guessed it: PEPPERDINE.

Phoenix was the home team today, and they played like it. We had Carson Jamison on the mound, and he'd been sharper. Carson may not be as great as he thinks he is—*nobody's* that great—but on a good day, if he pays attention to our catcher, Nick Cosimo, he's effective. Carson throws strikes and mixes his pitches. Today, though, his control was suspect. He walked two in the first inning, two in the second, and the leadoff hitter in the third.

Walks are almost never good, but a team like Phoenix will eat you up if you give them base runners. Example: Bottom of the first. First batter walks and then steals second on what turns out to be the third strike on batter two. Nick throws to the base, but even with his powerful arm it isn't close. Third batter drags a perfect bunt down the first baseline. He legs it out, and now there are runners on the corners with one out.

The next batter flies to left, deep enough that left fielder Darius McKay can't keep the runner on third from tagging up and scoring. He throws to second to keep the other runner at first. But Carson walks the next guy, so there are runners on first and second. With two out, Carson hangs a curve that gets lined into right. The lead runner scores, the other one goes to third, and there are once again runners on the corners. When the next batter pops up to the infield, they're done. But we've given up two runs that really boiled down to Carson's lack of control.

Meanwhile, Troy Scott was rolling for Phoenix. Darius got a leadoff single in the first and stole second, but the next three batters struck out. In the second, with one out, I managed a single on a bloop fly. Then Zack Waddell struck out. Nick was up, and Scott blew two heaters by him for strikes. Nick took a time-out and then got back in the box. On the next pitch I spotted—and fortunately Nick did too—Scott squeezing his glove twice around his pitching hand before he started his stretch. Nick waited and parked the changeup in the left-field seats.

But we played catch-up all morning. After seven innings the Eagles were up 5–3, and Scott was still ringing our guys up, including yours truly in the fifth.

I led off the eighth, looking for the fastball. With the game near the end, some power pitchers get impatient and just start throwing as hard as they can to get it over with. I guessed right and lined the ball deep to the gap in right. It was a triple. Zack then flew out to center, and I tagged up easily to score. 5–4.

But that was it. We couldn't make up the difference. The Eagles were in the finals. We'd be playing for third.

CHAPTER 5

"Danny, that was a hard-fought game. I'm sorry you fell a little short."

It was the fat guy in the now very rumpled white suit. He had sweat stains under his arms and across his back, and he was still wiping his head with the hankie. He had come down to the dugout right after we'd shaken hands with the Eagles. He'd had to wait a minute, though. PEPPERDINE had arrived first.

"Sorry, Danny," she said. "Nice triple, though." It turned out her name was Kayla. She was a freshman communications major at the college she had advertised so excellently. She lived with her parents in Malibu, just a mile from school. I hoped we'd talk a while, but she saw White Suit waiting and just said, "I'll be at the game tomorrow" before she left.

The suit had a strong accent, maybe German, and introduced himself as Jack Strauss. "Actually, that's my name for doing business in America," he said. "My name at home is Joachim Strausshoffer. I spoke with your father yesterday."

"Yes, sir, he mentioned you'd be here."

"Good, good. Look, it's getting hot out here. You probably want to get back to the hotel and clean up. I wanted to talk to you about a business proposition."

"Business? Me?"

"Yes, yes. You can meet me maybe for a late lunch? I'll be in the restaurant at your hotel at 1:30."

"Sure."

As he walked away, I noticed he had a black shoulder bag with a logo on it—a gold cat inside the letter *O*.

I found the team bus and settled in by a window for the short ride back to the hotel. In a few seconds I had almost dozed off— the game catching up with me—when I was suddenly aware of Coach Harris in the seat next to me.

"Hey, Danny," he said. "Good game. Who was the guy in the suit?"

I told him the man's name and that he said something about business. "I'll know more this afternoon," I said. "The guy knows my dad."

"Did you notice the man purse?" the coach said.

"Yeah."

"The logo—the cat?—that's Ocelot. A German company. They make high-end sports gear. They're big in Japan. Anyway, keep your nose clean."

. . .

Back at the hotel I showered and changed. I waved at Shotaro and the Xbox he'd become obsessed with playing and laid down for a quick rest. Good thing I set my phone alarm—when it went off I was well on my way to a long nap.

The restaurant was separate from the dining room where we had team meals. This place was all crystal and linen tablecloths, with deep green carpeting and a view of the pool. It seemed like everyone in the room was fit and tanned and ridiculously good-looking, except for Jack Strauss, who waved to me from a seat by the window. I made my way over and he stood up, extending a pudgy hand. I ordered a $20 burger and a soda; Strauss got a salad with fruit and goat cheese and a bottle of Perrier. I was noticing this stuff so I could tell Mel about it later.

"Well, Danny," Strauss said at last, "let me tell you about my business. I represent Ocelot. We make all kinds of sports equipment and gear for all kinds of athletes, from amateurs to elite players like yourself. And we market all over the world. We are just now beginning to do business in America."

I nodded.

"For some time, we've been watching the amateur baseball scene here, and we've noticed you. I'm not just trying to flatter you, Danny, but you have a great deal of talent, and something else. A kind of flair. And you're likeable. When you made that catch the other night, people were impressed, but I think they were also happy for you. Anyway, we certainly noticed how you could help our company, and vice-versa."

"How?"

Strauss smiled. "Suppose," he said, "suppose when you made that catch you had been wearing some kind of gear with our Ocelot logo. How many people do you think saw that catch?"

"Lots, I guess. It was on—"

"One hundred and twenty-three million people in North and South America."

Our food arrived, and Strauss went on.

"You will make more plays like that, Danny. I know you will. You have the skills.

So the next time you do something people notice, Ocelot wants to share in the attention."

"You want me to wear your stuff."

"Exactly. And in addition to all the gear you want—well, I've spoken to your father and he's very happy about your opportunity— Ocelot would provide quite generous financial compensation."

"I don't think I can take money without turning pro. If I want to go to college . . ."

Strauss held up a hand. "If you want to go to college, that's great. We would simply pay your father, who will hold the money in trust until eligibility is no longer an issue. If you go pro, great. If not, when you finish playing amateur ball you'll have a very respectable amount of cash to start whatever career you choose."

Wow. Strauss's offer sounded pretty good. Finally, I said, "Thanks, Mr. Strauss. I'm interested. I need to talk to my dad before I make any agreements, though."

"Of course, of course!" Strauss beamed. "He and I will be in touch."

CHAPTER 6

On the way back to my room, my head was spinning. I'm a good player, I know that. But why wouldn't Strauss go after someone like Sammy Perez? Our right fielder was definitely headed for the pros, everybody knew that. What was the word Strauss used? *Flair.* What did he mean by that? I decided to rest on it. My head barely touched the pillow before I was out. When I woke up three hours later, it was time for our team meal.

Not everyone on the team eats supper together on these trips. Sometimes players will hang out with their families. But the coaches are always there, and it's relaxing. No heavy baseball discussions. They save the serious stuff for practices.

I found a spot next to Coach Washington. We hadn't spoken since the night of The Catch, but he seemed all smiles, like he didn't remember that conversation.

"What's up, Danny?" he said. And I just told him. About Strauss, the deal, everything.

"Wow," he said. "All that attention must feel pretty good."

I told him I guessed it did.

"You might have a problem with the logo deal, though."

"How?"

"You ever noticed the star on the back of your cap and the shoulder of your jersey?"

"Yeah, I suppose it's a brand or something."

"Or something. The Runners get all their gear from Pop's Stars Sporting Goods."

"The giant sports store in Vegas?" I was surprised. I'd been in the store a few times.

"Actually three giant stores. You know Pop Mancini?"

"The old guy who comes to practices and hangs out?"

Wash chuckled. "Yeah, him. That 'old guy' owns Pop's Stars. He's been supplying the Runners with uniforms and equipment since before you were born. He started out with a little storefront downtown; now he's got three of those megastores in Vegas and the 'burbs."

"I thought he was just a fan. A retired guy with time on his hands."

"Oh, he's a fan all right. The man has always loved baseball. And Pop knows everyone in the game. A couple of years ago he showed up at practice with Tommy Lasorda. He's not retired, though. Still runs his stores."

"So . . . the logo? You think he'd have a problem with Ocelot?"

"Maybe, maybe not. His agreement with the Runners goes back before my time. Probably based on a handshake. That's a matter of pride with Pop. He's as good as his word."

"But I'm not covering up Pop's stars, just adding a few things of my own."

"I can't tell you if there's any problem on the business side. That's probably between Pop and Ocelot, and anyone who knows Pop knows he can take of himself when it comes to the competition.

"In Pop's eyes, though, those stars are about more than business."

"What are they about?" This Pop guy sort of sounded like a sap.

"Like three seasons ago at the banquet, the team gave Pop an award, a plaque, you know? For thirty years of backing the Runners."

"Yeah?"

"Pop gave a little speech. He said the biggest reward for him was seeing his stars on generations of young players and knowing he'd helped them be a part of the game."

That was definitely sappy. "I still don't get why he'd object to—"

"Because Pop *earned* that space. He didn't

just buy it. And now some new kid on the block wants to act like he can stand in the same space, like he's equal."

I guess Wash had a point, but Ocelot was offering me something unique. I needed to think about it. I hoped Pop wouldn't be a problem for Strauss.

. . .

When my phone rang that night, it was Dad.

"Danny! How's my boy?"

"I'm good, Dad. How are you?"

"Excellent. I heard you had lunch with our friend Strauss."

"Yeah. I'm still trying to sort that out."

"What's to sort out? It's a great opportunity!"

"You think so?"

"Absolutely! Look, Danny, since that catch the other night, you're a star! Seize the moment!"

"Do you know Pop Mancini?"

"Everybody in Vegas knows Pop. He's got more money than—"

"I know. Coach Washington told me he has an agreement with the Runners. It's like he's our exclusive supplier or something."

"Supplier, yes. Exclusive? I don't think so. Look at your glove. It says Mizuno. No one has a problem with that. Anyway, this isn't about taking anything away from Pop's Stars. It's about adding something for Danny. Grab it, son."

"So I wouldn't be breaking any kind of rule?"

"Nope, I've worked it all out with Strauss."

"Okay, Dad, if you think it's the right thing ..."

"Great. Now who do you play tomorrow?"

"Oakland."

"The Bay Bombers! All right, you rest up. I'll give Strauss a call, tell him we're cool, and we'll make plans when you're back in Vegas. Go get 'em, son!"

Despite the nap before dinner I slept fine that night. Maybe I shouldn't have.

CHAPTER 7

The consolation game between the Las Vegas Roadrunners and the Oakland Bay Bombers was scheduled for the morning. The Phoenix Eagles would play under the lights in the final, against a team from Mexico.

We had never played the Bombers, so we were eager to hear Coach Harris's scouting report on the bus to the ballpark.

"Listen up, guys," he began. "Today you'll be looking in the mirror. The Bombers look a lot like us. They're strong at every position; they've got some serious power and a couple of all-stars. It's all going to come down to execution.

"If we have an advantage, it might be our speed, but more important is our hustle. I've talked to some of the other coaches, and they said that every now and then the Bombers get lazy. But we can't count on that, and anyway, you could say the same about us.

"Their pitcher. Bart Kenner. He's not the fastest guy you'll face, but he's got good command of three pitches: fastball, slider, and a twelve-to-six curve that can make you look very silly at the plate. Watch for the fastball—it's hittable if he doesn't locate it just right."

A lot of times when we arrive at the field, the fans and family members there will pat us on the back or shout "Good luck!" Today, however, something truly weird happened. Among the fans were what looked like a Little League team—a dozen ten- to twelve-year-old boys in uniforms with leopard-spotted shirts and hats with big Ocelot logos on them. When they saw me, they ran over and crowded around, holding up pens and baseballs. "Danny! Danny Manuel! Will you sign?"

I was thinking, *What the . . . ?* when I noticed, a few yards away, two guys with important video cameras. What could I do? I signed the baseballs. But I could feel my teammates staring. When we got to the dugout, Nellie came up to me.

"Man, what was *that* all about?"

"I'm not really sure," was all I said.

During warm-ups I spotted Kayla in her usual spot behind the plate. She waved, and I waved back. And before long, here came Jack Strauss, water bottle in hand, settling down behind the dugout in the third row. In front of him was Team Ocelot. When Mr. Strauss saw me he stood up and waddled down to the rail, motioning me to come over.

"Hi, Danny, I just wanted to wish you—" His phone beeped.

He looked at the ID and gestured for me to hold on a second.

"Yes?" he said. "What? Who does this Pop Mancini think he is? Ten percent? What a joke! Okay, I'll meet with him. Maybe he thinks he's hot stuff in Vegas, but he doesn't know who he's dealing with!"

Strauss put his phone back in his purse. I'd never seen him upset before.

"Sorry, Danny. This guy Pop Mancini is trying to squeeze us. He says that the Roadrunners' uniforms and the *Roadrunners themselves* are his advertising space! He has no problem with the Ocelot logo being displayed on 'his space,' but he wants ten percent of our profits on any gear we sell in Nevada. Can you believe it?"

"What are you going to do?"

"Sue him, if it comes to that. I'm going to meet him tomorrow and let him know just where we stand. Anyway, that's not your worry. I just wanted to wish you good luck."

. . .

We were the home team today, and Coach started Jonas Creeley. I once heard Nellie say that everyone likes Jonas except Jonas. And that kind of pinpointed the problem, when there was one: his confidence.

Jonas had mad skills: a live fastball that tailed away from righties and handcuffed lefties, an undetectable change, and a wicked slider. When he was locating, Jonas was nearly unhittable. In fact, he had thrown a no-no for the Runners last season. But when Jonas started slow or someone got to him, he would get down on himself. He'd start muttering things like, "Jonas, you idiot!" He'd start walking batters and finally get wild. For Nick, our catcher, Jonas was high maintenance. The rest of us just prayed he would start strong.

Fortunately, that was the case today. He no-hit the Bombers for the first three innings, with three Ks. In the same span we had only one hit, but it was a home run with a man on base, hit by yours truly. Kenner had walked Sammy. Carlos "Trip" Costas had grounded wide to short, so they had to play at first. And I guessed fastball on the first pitch and there it was, belt-high over the plate. I don't have the kind of power that Sammy and Nellie do, but over the fence is over the fence, and that's where I put it.

As I rounded third base, I saw Team O doing a sort of mini-wave and shaking leopard-spotted towels. One of the video guys was shooting them, and the other one was shooting me as I crossed the plate and got congratulated in the dugout. I shot a smile at Kayla, who was jumping up and down and cheering.

After that it seemed like our team could do no wrong. Jonas finally gave up a hit—a double—in the sixth, but the Bombers stranded their runner. I singled in the fourth and doubled in the seventh, driving in runs both times. By the eighth we were up 6–0.

But then things started to go south. Jonas walked the first two batters and gave up singles to the next two. Shotaro started working in the pen. With the score 6–2, men on first and third, Jonas threw wild. Now it was 6–3 with a man on second. Jonas was talking to himself, and when he walked the next batter, Coach yanked him.

Shotaro struck out the first batter he faced, but the second singled: 6–4, runners on first and third. Then, disaster. The batter hit a short fly to Darius in left. The runner on third tagged, and Darius threw to the plate—a perfect strike. Nick had the plate blocked, but the runner slammed into him. Nick held. The runner was out. But our catcher was down.

CHAPTER 8

*P*layers and coaches from the dugout and the field converged on the plate. It was a clean play, no question. But Nick was the brains of our team on the field, besides being one of the best-liked guys on the roster.

By the time I got to the plate Nick was already sitting up, but he was only half there. The trainers took off his mask and helmet, wiped his forehead with some wet towels, and felt his head. They let him rest where he was for maybe five minutes, and then they gently helped him up and led him into the clubhouse.

Our guys—Darius, Gus Toomey, and Nellie—went down in order in the bottom of the eighth. In the ninth, Shotaro looked lost. He walked the first batter, who promptly stole second. The second batter doubled in the run. The next guy at the plate was their cleanup hitter, a lefty, and he drove Sammy to the wall in right. Sammy made the catch, but the tying run was on third.

The next play was almost identical, except this time the tag-up tied the game. Shotaro was really unnerved, and Nick wasn't there to calm him down. On the first pitch, the next batter ripped a line drive down the third baseline, but somehow Nellie snagged it for the last out.

It was the bottom of the ninth inning and the score was tied at 6. Sammy was at the plate, Trip was on deck, and I was in the circle. Sammy got to 3–2 quickly, and then he fouled off three pitches before he connected. Their left fielder played it well off the fence, but

Sammy's speed got him to second standing up.

You could make an argument that Sammy is the best player on our team. He'll probably go pro some day. But once in a while he'll get overconfident. Like this time. With no one out and Trip at the plate, Sammy decided to steal third base on the first pitch. I heard Wash swear. The element of surprise was no match for their catcher's arm. Sammy was out, and he hung his head on the way back to the dugout.

Trip worked the count to 3–2 like Sammy had done but then got called out on a pitch that looked like it was around his ankles. He looked at the umpire in disbelief and then said something quietly that got him thrown out of the game in record time. Whatever Trip had said, it couldn't have been as bad as the stuff his dad, Julio, was yelling from the stands. Maybe the ump didn't hear him.

Now I was up with two out. I'd been watching the pitcher—a reliever now—and he had thrown a fastball on the first pitch to almost every batter he'd faced. So I was dug in dead red when the ump called time and the Bombers' coach motioned to the bullpen for a new guy. Man!

I watched him warm up, but that was no help. He was an average-sized guy—even a little chubby. He didn't look overpowering. While I was waiting, Wash came over.

"Junk," he said. "Wait on the pitch as long as you can."

"Junk" was right. The first pitch was a floating curve that had *yard* written all over it. But I waited like Wash said, and just as it got to me it jumped up about six inches. Ball one, high. The second one moved late, too, in on my hands. I fought it off foul. One and one. On the third pitch he made a mistake. It was a floater like the first one, but I waited and it just stayed right there. So I pulled the trigger.

I didn't even look to see where it went. I knew from the feel of the ball on the bat and the noise of the fans that it was gone. When I got to home, the team was waiting for me. My team, the Roadrunners, and little Team Ocelot in those spotted shirts. And Kayla, with a long, hard hug. It was a moment, I have to say.

I made plans to watch the final with Kayla in the evening. It was a good game: Phoenix beat the Mexican team, winning the way they usually did: bunts, stolen bases, timely singles, and stingy pitching.

After the game they gave out the trophies. The Runners were third overall, and we all ran up together to get the cup. Then came the surprise that ended the day. They called my name on the loudspeaker. I was voted MVP of the tournament! The noise, the excitement, and the people pounding me on the back put me in a kind of daze as I went up to accept the plaque.

Before the Palm, I hadn't experienced the hero thing. Now I was discovering that I liked it—a lot.

CHAPTER 9

As I walked through the hotel lobby with the rest of the Runners on the way to our bus to the airport, I felt a firm, sweaty grip on my shoulder.

"Danny! Just a minute!"

I turned, startled, to see Mr. Strauss towering next to me. I wondered how I possibly could have missed him.

"Mr. Strauss?"

"I know you're on your way home, Danny.

I just wanted to give this to you before you left." Mr. Strauss handed me a sheet of paper with something typed on it.

"It's your commercial!"

I couldn't believe it. My own *commercial*! Ocelot was obviously the best thing that had ever happened to me.

"We've already got it made. It will be posted on the Internet today. Next week you'll see it on TV!"

I didn't know what to say, so I just yelled, "Awesome, Mr. Strauss!" and raced to catch up with the team.

On the bus, I read the screenplay for the commercial:

Intro: Faint guitar instrumental.

Young blond boy in spotted shirt, Ocelot logo on black cap: "Danny, will you sign my baseball?"

Suddenly, whole team of kids similarly attired: "Danny! Danny!"

Cut to Danny and crack of the bat.

Cut to cheering Ocelot-clothed kids waving towels.

Cut to Danny crossing the plate, crowd crazy.

Cut to Danny in interview: "Just, you know, get it."

Cut to video: The Catch.

Voiceover: "There's no way. The Eagles win. No, wait! Oh. My. Gosh! Did you see that?"

Danny interview: "Just, you know, get it."

Cut to video of MVP Award.

Voiceover: "And the MVP of the Palm Springs Invitational Amateur Baseball Series: the Las Vegas Roadrunners' Danny Manuel."

Danny: "Thank you. I feel like Superman today."

Zoom in on logo.

Silent slow-motion of The Catch.

Danny voice over: "Just, you know, get it."

Ocelot logo to Fade Out.

It was awesome. I couldn't wait for everyone to see it.

. . .

When I got back home Dad and Sal were there to welcome me. A week later, Mel stopped by. Her season was over and school was out, but she was going to play in Japan and Europe over the summer. She was here just for me, and knowing that made me feel great.

"So," she said when we finally got a chance to talk alone, "how is all this hitting you?"

"I like it a lot," I said. "It's kind of cool to think of little kids looking up to me and stuff. Did you see the commercial?"

She looked at me a little funny when I said that, but she went on. "Yeah, it's cool. But what do you think of this 'arrangement' with Ocelot? Dad seems happy."

"You know, since the TV stuff I've been getting mail. Last week some girl proposed."

Mel laughed. "Are you going to accept?"

"No, I'll wait a while. Consider my options, ya know?"

"Where is all this going, then, little brother?"

"Well, I talked to Mr. Strauss. We're doing some more commercials. And figuring out how to make the logo more visible during games. That footage is really valuable for promos if we can show the brand."

"Wow, Danny, you are growing your marketing vocabulary."

"Thank you," I laughed. "I think. The deal is our team has a verbal contract with Pop's Stars Sporting Goods—"

"Love that place!"

"Yeah. So we wear their logo on our gear. But the lawyers think—"

"Lawyers?"

"Licensing guys. They think that as long as Pop's logo is visible, there's no problem showing other brands as well. Pop's is a retailer, not a manufacturer. So we won't touch his stars, but we'll use other opportunities for visibility."

"Hey, if you decide to leave baseball, maybe you can go into law."

"Well," I grinned, "if I do, law school is paid for."

. . .

With all the marketing stuff and our next series of games, I had a big couple of weeks.

It was crazy busy. With practices and Ocelot stuff I didn't have much down time. I texted with Kayla in my spare moments. We had a tournament in LA in a few weeks, and I was starting to think about her—to think about us—a lot. Maybe we had a future.

Future. That was the biggest thing on my mind then.

"You make your future now," Mr. Strauss told me. "Perception is reality. You want to play in the pros, get the media talking about you. This is the foundation. People learn who you are, they see you play, and doors open. These days it's not enough to be good. You need to be . . . attractive."

CHAPTER 10

Since the Palm, the Runners had good news. Nick, our catcher, was back in action. Apparently he was only shaken up in the collision in Palm Springs. We had a couple of practices in Vegas. Then we went up by bus to a weekend series in Carson City. The Carson City Capitals are a good team, especially at home. The plan was we'd play them both Saturday and Sunday afternoon, with a Sunday-night game if necessary.

On the highway, we were a caravan. The team bus was followed by team family vehicles, some of them big RVs that probably cost more than the bus. Carson's folks had one the size of a yacht, with a satellite dish on top and a name painted on the back: *Ship of the Desert*. Once we actually had a team party—you're talking thirty-some people—inside that RV.

This trip one of the floats in our parade was a leopard-spotted van with an Ocelot logo on the side.

I think it was when we pulled up to the field on Saturday that it really hit me: I was a star. When I got off the bus there were kids chanting, "Dan-ee! Dan-ee!" Of course a certain sports gear company was on the scene handing out free T-shirts to everyone: leopard spots and the Ocelot logo, like the one I was wearing under my jersey. They also had balloons with the same spots and logo, and every little kid seemed to be holding one. Last but not least, they had 8x10 glossy photos of me making The Catch. They all wanted me to sign their photos.

On Saturday things went our way. Carson was in a groove, our power guys were hitting, and I handled a lot of business—in more ways than one—in center field. Mr. Strauss and I had worked out that I'd unbutton my jersey a little when I was in the field so the Ocelot T-shirt would show for the fans—and the cameras, of which the company now had four placed at different spots around the field.

With one out in the sixth, the Capitals' catcher drove one hard to the fence in center. I caught up with it, though, and grabbed it over my head. The crowd yelled and waved the spotted balloons, and I just held up the ball for a minute and grinned, showing the shirt, before I remembered there was a runner on second.

Sure enough, he had tagged up and was streaking for third. I gunned it in towards third, but Trip cut it off. Even if the throw had gone to the base, Nellie would have had to handle it on two hops. Better to let the guy take third.

Uh-oh, my bad. As it happened, the next guy grounded out, so the runner was stranded. Still I could feel the glares of my teammates and Wash as I returned to the dugout. All Wash said as I passed him was, "Your shirt's unbuttoned," but his tone said a lot more.

Whatever. I drove in a run that inning, and we eventually beat the Caps 5–2. No one spoke to me on the bus ride back to the hotel. Nellie stopped for a minute on the way to his seat and looked at me like he was going to say something, but then he just raised his eyebrows and passed by. Shotaro was in the seat next to me, hooked up to his earplugs and iPod.

"Is it a little chilly in here?" I said to him, but of course he didn't hear.

Baseball—heck, all sports—is funny. One day you're totally, effortlessly focused; the next day you're flat. You'd think, since a baseball team carries a couple of dozen different players, that the individual ups and downs would even out. But it doesn't always work that way; sometimes the whole team bottoms out at once.

That's what happened to us Sunday afternoon. The Caps weren't bad. Their pitcher was steady and their infield was scooping up everything hit on the ground. Which was part of our problem. Almost everything we hit was on the ground. In nine innings, we had three hits and the Caps had turned three double plays. Jonas pitched well for us, and he deserved better. But our cold bats made him the loser, 3–0.

The guys were quiet at supper. We'd lost something, and we didn't know where to find it. At dessert, though, Coach Harris stood and spoke. He actually seemed pretty upbeat.

"Look guys," he said, "once in a while you're going to have a game like that. Sometimes you can't tell why. It looked to me like everyone was hustling. When I see that, I'm not too discouraged. And the good thing is, we had it to spend. We can still go home winners tonight, okay?"

Nellie spoke up. "We will, Coach. Right, guys?"

The leader thing. Coach has it. Nellie has it. And we all trusted it. Somehow we snapped out of our funk. At least that's how it felt.

CHAPTER *11*

When we got to the ballpark I was in for a surprise. Dad was there, along with Sal, and they were talking with Mr. Strauss.

I ran over and hugged Dad, who seemed to be in a great mood.

"I have a good feeling about this game," he said. "Right, Jack?"

"Without a doubt, sir. Danny, we're shooting a new advertisement this series. I think you'll love it. Great job showing the colors yesterday—just what we need. Here, I brought you something."

He reached in his man purse and pulled out a spotted doo-rag with the Ocelot logo on the top.

"I've been talking with your father about incentives. We pay a certain amount for you to wear our gear; you know that. But every time our cameras spot the logo in a play situation, there's a bonus."

"A bonus?"

"It's a great deal, son," Dad beamed. "Just do what you . . . do." And he winked and nodded at the doo-rag.

I turned to Mr. Strauss.

"Did you meet with Pop Mancini?" I asked.

"Why yes," Strauss muttered. "It turns out Mr. Mancini is well connected in this area. He's friends with judges, casino owners, you name it. An outsider like Ocelot would have a difficult, expensive time getting a favorable decision in a lawsuit in Las Vegas."

"What will you do?"

"Pay him what he asks, for now."

My dad looked concerned. "That payoff isn't coming out of Danny's earnings, is it?"

Strauss put this hand on my dad's shoulder, "Oh, no, no. We'll pass the extra cost along to the consumer. We'll simply raise our prices by eleven percent. It's cheaper than going to court."

"Well, that's reasonable," my dad commented.

I heard Coach calling in the players.

"Okay! Team's calling me. See ya later!"

"Good luck, son!" yelled my dad.

The renewed confidence we'd felt at dinner was tested in the very first inning. We had gone hitless in the top, and Carson struck out their first two batters. But then Bo "Beast" Bronsky, their first baseman, came to the plate. Six-four, around 240, Beast looks about twenty-five. He was first and foremost a football player—a defensive tackle who was being recruited by colleges like Texas and Nebraska. But he was a good enough athlete to play for most traveling teams, and his power at the plate was legend. The Caps had played an exhibition last season at AT&T Park, where the San Francisco Giants play, and Beast put one in McCovey Cove.

Carson made him fan on two curveballs and then thought he could slip a fastball by for strike three. Wrong. Beast walloped that pitch over the light poles in right and literally out of sight. When the yelling stopped, you could hear a car alarm going off somewhere in the distance.

Their cleanup batter tagged one too, toward center, but not as far as I thought at first. I sprinted about five strides, then looked over my shoulder and saw that I could come in a few steps and wait for it to come down. I caught it for the third out. Then I whipped off my cap so folks could see the spotted doo-rag on my run back to the dugout. Ka-ching!

It turned out the Beast hadn't scared us for long. In the top of two, our first three batters—Sammy, Trip, and I—singled. Zack popped up. But then Nick, just to prove he was back, went yard on the first pitch. It was 4–1.

Carson settled down in the bottom of three, getting the side in order. Things were looking good. But in the fourth, the Caps brought in a new pitcher and our bats went quiet. It was just like earlier in the day— ground balls. Meanwhile, the Caps nibbled away—a run each in the fourth, the seventh, and the eighth.

We came to bat with the score tied in the top of the ninth. Sammy, leading off, was ready for the pitch when suddenly the catcher called time and headed to the mound. He spoke to the pitcher a moment, and then he waved to their dugout. Out popped their coach, who trotted in for a conference on the mound. A minute later a trainer was out there as well.

It was something with the pitcher's throwing hand. Probably a blister. Whatever it was, the coach called for a reliever. From our point of view, anyone new was a sign of hope. On the reliever's first pitch, though, Sammy fanned. On the second he tried to check up, but the ump said he swung. Strike two.

Pitch three was a ball, high, and on the next delivery Sammy grounded hard to the shortstop.

Sammy never gives up, though, and the speed he was showing down the line must have made the shortstop nervous. He hurried and bobbled the ball just a beat as he grabbed it to throw, and Sammy was safe at first.

Trip Costas walked. Sometimes Trip doesn't seem very aggressive at the plate, but he has some of the best eyes on the team. The pitcher was throwing breaking stuff and just missing.

My turn. I put on my cap—I'd had it off in the on-deck circle—and batting helmet and stood in the box. I was looking to just make contact; with Sammy's speed, he might score on a single. But when this big, slow pitch came in right over the plate, I had to take a rip. I just about fell down I swung so hard. But I missed it by a foot. I heard some people in the stands laughing, and even the umpire chuckled a little when he said, "That was a curveball, son."

I figured the pitcher made me look so bad on that pitch that he'd try it again, so I was taking on the next one, which turned out to be a knee-high fastball right down the pipe. Who was this guy?

Same pitch next time, but just low for ball one. Then another big curve. It was all I could do to take that one, but it broke down into the dirt at the last minute. I stepped out of the box to remind myself what I wanted to do. Just make contact. A short swing.

Here came the windup, the pitch. I took a short, crisp stroke and caught . . . air. Sometime in my follow-through the ball crossed the plate. Strike three. But that wasn't all. For some reason Trip had started for second. Sammy was on his way to third! The catcher gunned it to third. Sammy was hung up, desperately trying to avoid a tag until Trip could get to second or back to first.

Trip decided on second and was on his way there when the third baseman tagged

Sammy and threw to second, now covered by the pitcher. Trip slid. Safe! I had just about triggered a triple play.

I wasn't feeling too good even then, but it got worse in the dugout. Wash was all over me.

"The hit and run was on, Danny!" he hissed. "Didn't you see the sign?"

I never looked for the sign. I was focused on saving the day all by myself.

CHAPTER 12

W e were still tied, though, and when Zack doubled to right center we were a run up. And that's how things stood when the Caps came up in the bottom of the ninth.

Coach had Shotaro on the mound to close things out, and he started steady. Their first hitter grounded to short. The next guy struck out.

Their third batter, though, just wouldn't go out. The count had gone to 3–2 when he started fouling everything Shotaro had. And Shotaro wanted him bad, because the guy on deck was none other than Beast Bronsky. But after six fouls, Shotaro lost the battle. He threw a ball outside, and the Caps had the winning run at the plate.

Walking the Beast was a no-brainer. Such a no-brainer that the Caps were well prepared. Despite Bronsky's awesome power, the leading RBI guy on the Caps was Tim Pesci. Because he hit right after Beast, he often came to the plate with men on base, and even though he wasn't as powerful, he was a better hitter than Bronsky.

The Caps put a pinch runner on first. Coach Harris signaled the outfield to come in to medium depth, in case a short single required a play at the plate. Nick went out to talk to Shotaro.

On the first pitch we got a scare. Pesci, a lefty, drilled one down the line about six inches outside the bag. The next two pitches were balls.

I can't explain it, but sometime during Shotaro's next delivery I got this weird feeling.

I don't even think it was in my head. It was more in my legs. When Pesci connected and the sinking line drive started to head my way, I was already moving forward.

Even though I was focused on the ball, I was aware of their lead runner scampering toward third, and I knew that I'd made the same mistake Wash had criticized before. I should have fielded it and tried for a play at the plate. It was too late, though. From the moment, maybe just before the moment, the bat hit the ball, I was committed: just get it.

I saw the spot ahead of me where the ball would hit the ground. It was just a race to see which of us would get there first. I dived for the spot, my glove stretched out in front, and felt the ball bury itself in the pocket. I heard the noise. I had it.

My hat came off all by itself on that play. I was pretty sure Dad and Mr. Strauss would be pleased.

CHAPTER *13*

*S*toryboard: Ocelot 2
000: Black screen
002: text white: See Spots
004: background gradual change to leopard
 spots
007: text black: See Spots Run
009: video Danny chasing fly
013: text on spots: See Spots Fly
015: video Danny leaping for catch
019: text on spots: See Spots Win

021: video Danny hoisted by teammates, crowd
    waving towels
025: logo black on spots
027: voiceover Danny: Just, you know, get it.
030: out.

Three days after the game, with the new commercial airing, the fan mail was piling in:

Yo! Dan the Man! You rule!

Dear Danny I saw you on TV and my bff thinks we would make a good couple. Write me? Ashley

Hey Danny, Saw the video and it's clear you can go places. I would like to offer my services as your agent/representative as you confront your undoubtedly many opportunities. Here's my cell number.

Hi Danny: I coach a Little League team here in Eldorado and I think you would be a great inspiration to my players. Would you be willing to stop in at one of our games or practices and say a few words?

I got interviewed on three local TV stations and sat in for an hour on LV's most popular sports talk radio show. I was signing autographs at every game, and people were even showing up at our practices to see me. At one point Coach Harris chased away an Ocelot video production crew that was trying to get footage of me in warm-ups.

I'll be honest. I could tell the rest of the team was getting tired of all the attention. And I'll be even more honest. I was loving it. I had the "Show Your Spots" move down to an art. Fly ball? I could lose the cap before the catch. In the dugout I always wore a big spotted towel over my shoulders.

One day Mr. Strauss presented me with three pairs of leopard-spotted baseball shoes. They were pretty sharp, I've gotta say. Mr. Strauss said they were selling like crazy. You could see them on billboards: just the shoes and the line "See Spots Run."

The shoes kind of brought things the team was feeling out in the open. The first time I wore them in practice Coach Harris called me over.

"Okay, Danny, what's with the shoes?"

"Part of my deal, Coach. Don't you like them?"

"I do not."

"Well . . ."

"Danny, why do you think we wear uniforms? I mean, instead of just whatever's comfortable?" He didn't wait for me to answer. "It's so we look alike. It makes us equal. Shows that we're a team."

"It's just shoes, Coach. I still wear the uniform."

"And the doo-rag. And the T-shirt and the towel. Danny, what those shoes say is, 'Yeah, I may be on a team, but I'm special.' Think about it."

Well, I thought about it, and I decided that, you know, I was special. Nobody else on the team had a product deal or their picture on billboards. In fact, I doubted anyone else on the team could make some of the plays I did. And make them with *flair*.

Anyway, shoes were personal. We all wore different brands, whatever felt best. It was just that everyone else wore boring black. Anyway,

Coach just said, "Think about it." He didn't say I couldn't wear them. That's why I was surprised when he benched me when I wore them to the next game.

CHAPTER *14*

Wash actually gave me the news. "Harris says players wear black shoes in games. Otherwise they don't play." They moved Darius to my position in center. The Runners lost by six runs—our pitching collapsed. I don't remember all the details. I do remember a moment in the seventh inning, though.

There were two out, we were in the field, and the batter hit a high pop fly to center. Darius hardly had to move, but while he waited for it to come down he took off his cap, waved it at the crowd, and tossed it aside.

As the guys came in they were all laughing and poking Darius like, "Good one!" Even the coaches were smiling. I thought, *Go ahead and laugh.* Fact is, we lost.

I thought Dad and Mr. Strauss would be upset when I told them I couldn't wear the shoes anymore. Instead they looked at each other and started smiling. "Don't worry, Danny," Mr. Strauss said after a while. "Ocelot makes black shoes too."

The next morning at breakfast Dad handed me the sports section of the *Las Vegas Sun*.

"Check it out, Danny," he said.

Coach Benches Star for Shoe Infraction

According to reports, Las Vegas Roadrunners Coach Scott Harris benched star center fielder Danny Manuel in yesterday's game for his wardrobe. Manuel, who has an agreement with Germany-based Ocelot Sports Ltd., came to the game wearing shoes with Ocelot's trademark

leopard spots and logo. Coach Harris
apparently saw red, not spots, when he
noticed the stand-out apparel and removed
Manuel from the lineup.

Neither the coach nor the player were
available for comment on the incident,
but Joachim Strausshoffer, Ocelot's North
American director of development, said
that Manuel will continue to wear Ocelot
shoes in the standard black model. "Ocelot
and Danny's fans want him to play,"
Strausshoffer said, explaining that he had
offered to supply the entire team with the
spotted shoes, but the coach had not responded.

Even with all the attention I had been
getting, I was surprised that a newspaper would
report on the shoes I was wearing. I wondered
what Harris would think when he saw the
article. I sort of hoped he didn't read the paper.

But the story got picked up nationally, and
it was all over the Internet. Within a week the
"See Spots Run" billboards had changed. They
still showed the shoes, but above them it said

"BANNED!" and underneath was a picture of my smiling face, followed by, "I can't wear them. But you can!"

Needless to say, sales of the spotted shoes went through the roof. I even read about a high school team in Idaho, the Jaguars, that made the shoes standard for the team.

As for me, I was back in the field in new black shoes with a small gold Ocelot logo on the heels. I could feel the tension, though. Coach Harris barely talked to me, and the same went for the rest of the team, except for Wash and Nellie, who always talked to everyone.

One day I caught up with Nellie after practice and asked him point blank, "Is Coach pissed at me?"

"Maybe a little," Nellie said. "You—well, your business partners—embarrassed him. But Coach doesn't hold a grudge, and he knows you're valuable. Give it some time, show you're a team player, and things will get back to normal." I had this talk with Nellie just before the team left for a weekend series in Los Angeles. I had no idea how *not* normal things were going to get.

CHAPTER 15

From Las Vegas to LA is about a four-hour drive, at least till you get into traffic. On Friday, after lunch, the bus took our team and our stuff to a spread-out resort and spa in Santa Monica, right by the marina. One thing about the Roadrunners thanks to backers like Alexander Jamison and Julio Costas, we always have spectacular accommodations. For a few of us, baseball was the only way we would ever lead this kind of life.

We arrived in the late afternoon. Not too long afterwards I got a text from Kayla: *It seems like 4ever. Can't wait 2 c u! I'm by the pool!*

We only had forty-five minutes till the team meal, so I threw on shorts and an Ocelot T-shirt and headed outside.

It turned out that saying "by the pool" was sort of like saying "at the mall." The glittering turquoise water covered an area the size of a football field, and there were hundreds of people sitting or lying around it on towels or chaise lounges. About half of the people seemed to be gorgeous women. I started wandering around, swamped in the smell of chlorine and coconut oil and squinting in the glare coming off the water—I'd forgotten my spotted sunglasses. But the T-shirt came through for me.

"Danny! Over here!"

Kayla was about twenty yards to my right, wearing a tiny white bikini and a killer tan and sitting on a blue-and-orange Pepperdine beach towel. She stood up to give me a big welcoming hug.

"Nice shirt!" she grinned.

I grinned back.

She motioned for me to sit down. "So," she said, "I heard about your shoe trouble. But I guess you're back on the team."

"Yeah, Coach isn't saying much, but he lets me play now."

"Is that spots company paying you a lot of money?"

"I don't really know. My dad handles the business stuff."

When I told her I could only hang out for a couple of minutes, she made a little fake-pout expression but said, "Okay, duty calls. But I'll be at the game tomorrow, promise!"

One more hug, and this time a kiss on the cheek, and I headed back to the hotel.

. . .

The team we were going to play called themselves the Chicago Blues. By reputation, they were the best team we'd been matched up against since the Eagles. Two of their pitchers were already being described as potential major leaguers, as was their catcher, a kid named Fritz Benson. Fritz was being compared to a young phenomenon who was making history at the moment as a rookie for the San Francisco Giants. Guys of that caliber don't play on teams where the rest of the cast is weak. We were going to have our hands full.

That night Mel called me, like she often did before a big tournament, to wish me luck. Of course, she wanted to know all about the shoe incident. When I started to complain about Coach being too strict, she said, "Well, I'm sorry it happened, but I can see his point."

"What?" I said. "When he leaves me out of the lineup because he doesn't like my shoes, he's hurting the team."

"What do you mean?"

"Look what happened," I said. "I got benched and we lost by six runs."

Mel was quiet for a moment, and then she said, "Danny, do you hear what you're saying?"

"What?"

"You're talking like you are the team. Even the best player on a team isn't indispensable. That's what teamwork is about."

I could see Mel wasn't sympathetic, so I changed the subject. "How are things with you?"

"Brushing up on my Japanese," she said. "It's just a couple of weeks till I'm over there. Hang on a second." I heard her talking to someone, and then she was back.

"Okay, bro. I gotta go. I just wanted to say: Go, Runners! And I hope you have a great series. I'll check in next week for all the details, okay?"

"Sounds good. Love you, sis."

I was rooming with Shotaro again. As I drifted off to sleep that night, I could see the glow from his video game. I thought about Kayla and hoped I could do something tomorrow that would really get her attention.

CHAPTER 16

*I*t happened in the sixth inning of our first
game. We were in the field. I'd long since
perfected my move with the cap, taking it off
to show the Ocelot doo-rag when I made a
catch. It's the move Darius made fun of in the
game I sat out, but I didn't care. According to
Mr. Strauss it was making me money, and I
couldn't see how it hurt anybody.

We played in the afternoon. I don't think
the sun shines any brighter than it does on

the coast in California. It was definitely bright and cloudless that day. Going into the sixth, we were behind 3–1. I had hit a double in my first at bat and scored on Nick's single, but Carson had given up a three-run homer to Fritz Benson in the third. Now he was up again, and we were all playing deep in the outfield.

On the third pitch Benson hit a fly ball a mile high, but in front of me. I had plenty of time to lift the cap, and I thought maybe I'd wave it to the crowd before the ball came down. This was becoming my signature move, which was why Darius's joke worked, but so what? Problem was, somewhere in that little routine, I lost sight of the ball.

That's not usually a problem. But it happens, cap tip or no. A good outfielder who loses the ball doesn't panic. Fielders have quick eyes, and on a high fly there's time to pick up the ball in flight. You're probably already in the right spot, you just need to see it.

But this time all I could see was the sun. I looked quickly to my right at Darius.

Sometimes your teammate will see you're in trouble and help you out. But Darius didn't seem to notice there was a problem, and there was no way I was going to yell for help. I was thinking, *Okay, if I lose this I want to keep it in front of me*, so I took two steps back.

. . .

The next thing I remember I was in the locker room and a trainer was shining a light in my eye. Wash was there, and Shotaro and Kayla. I was on my back on a table, and I had a killer headache. I tried to sit up and the trainer pushed back on my shoulders. "Just relax, Danny, just relax. There's a doctor on the way."

"What do you mean?" I said. "I'm supposed to catch the ball. Here it comes!" I saw lights flashing. My head throbbed, and I felt like I was going to throw up. And then I did throw up, into a bucket the trainer was holding for me. I was embarrassed. Like I really wanted Kayla to see me puking.

Then another guy appeared. He had short gray hair, a black mustache, and thick glasses. The doctor, I guessed.

"Well," I heard him say, as if he was very far away, "it's at least a concussion. We'd better take him in for a CAT scan."

Every now and then I could hear the crowd out on the field. I didn't know who they were cheering for. And when I looked around for Kayla, she was gone.

It's hard at this point to sort out what I actually remember from what people have told me since. I did indeed go to the hospital. I had indeed suffered a concussion. The ball I lost in the sun had hit me on the right temple, right above my eye. I've seen photos since; they're not pretty.

Concussions are dangerous. Not just when they happen, but for a long time afterwards. They happen when a blow of some kind makes your brain bang around inside its cage—your skull. A little baseball falling from a height can pack a wallop, I learned.

The Roadrunners beat the Blues in the

series. More on that later. But the play where I got injured was pretty transparent on video. You saw a guy waiting for an easy catch, then grinning and tipping his hat to the crowd, then suddenly faltering, looking around in a panic until the baseball knocked him flat-out cold. I looked like an idiot.

CHAPTER 17

They kept me in the hospital for four days. When I got out, the team had gone home. But Dad, Mel, and Sal had all rushed to LA the minute they heard I was hurt. They all kept me company until I got out. On Thursday we drove back to Vegas, and during the drive I learned what had happened in the series.

When the ball hit me—well, when it bounced off my head—Darius recovered it and threw to the infield. Thanks to his quick reaction, I was charged with only a one-base error. There was a ten-minute delay until they took me off the field. Then Carson pitched us out of the inning. It was still 3–1.

Coach moved Darius to center and put Dave Teller in left. Darius came up in the next inning with Nick on base and parked one in center field. That tied the game, and the Runners went on to win 6–3 on a three-run ninth that included another hit—a triple—by Darius.

Game two on Sunday was rained out, a rare occurrence in LA, but the skies cleared in the evening and the Runners took a 2–0 lead right away on a homer by Sammy. Darius, leading off, had walked and stolen second, so he was the other run.

Both pitchers settled down after that, and Carson had a shutout going into the ninth. He gave up three doubles in that inning, though, and the Blues came back to tie.

In the tenth, our first guy walked and the next guy—guess who, Darius McKay— doubled. Then, with one out, Nellie hit a fly ball to deep center. It was caught, but Darius tagged up and scored! He just blew past third and into home. The throw wasn't even close. There was an element of surprise, but no one else on our team, or most teams for that matter, could have pulled it off.

Darius wasn't through. With two out and one on in the bottom of the tenth, he climbed the fence to rob Fritz Benson of a walk-off homer. Carson retired the last Blue, so the Runners won 3–2 and Darius had his biggest game ever for the team. It was extra sweet for him, too, since he had grown up in LA and had a lot of friends in the stands.

"Wow," I joked after Mel gave me the details. "I guess I better get back to work, or Darius will have my job." Instead of smiling, she looked down at the floor for a second and then at Dad.

"Son," he said without looking at me, "concussions take time for recovery. So there's a rule. You won't be able to play, or even practice, for at least six weeks. After that you need a doctor's okay."

That just kind of hung in the air for a few seconds while I did a quick calculation in my aching head.

"That's almost the rest of the season!"

"Danny," Mel said, putting her hand on my arm, "we're lucky to have you with us and to know you'll be okay. Baseball can wait."

. . .

Over the next week I learned why the league had a concussion rule. I'd be feeling perfectly fine, desperate to start playing, when out of the blue my head would start spinning. Sometimes I'd get these bad headaches and my vision would blur. Once I puked. That first week I also learned something else, via email:

Danny, how are you?! Darius told me you won't be able to play any more this year! Bummer! :(*At least your team won in LA. Darius was amazing, you probably heard. He's a really nice guy, though. We got to talking, turns out we know some of the same people here. Anyway, get well soon! Your friend, K*

It was looking like Darius had inherited more than my fielding position. If I had any doubts, they were gone by the second week, when I got a call from Mr. Strauss.

"Ah, Danny! How's the recovery?"

"Pretty good, mostly."

"That's great. See, I called to tell you Ocelot is sponsoring another member of your team, Darius McKay."

"Great," I said, clueless. "That's two of us. If you get a few more, maybe Coach Harris will let us wear those spotted shoes."

"Haha! Well, I wish we had the budget. Actually, I mean we're sponsoring only Darius now. Sorry, it's a business decision . . . since you won't be playing. We have to keep the brand out there in front of people, you know."

I think it was the day of that call that I threw up.

CHAPTER *18*

D espite all of the bad news, I didn't spend
all my time moping around the house
and feeling sorry for myself. And during this
time I started finding out who my real friends
were. As soon as I got back to Vegas, every
guy on the team—even Darius—called me
up or stopped by to wish me the best. Nice,
considering I'd been putting myself ahead of
the team and hurt myself in the process of
showing off. (A fact not missed, by the way, by

the media. Sports Center included the play in a collection of bloopers, hastening to add that I wasn't permanently hurt and they wished me the best.)

Nellie called the day after I heard from Mr. Strauss. When I told him what happened, he said, "Danny, do you really miss the spots thing?"

And the fact was, I didn't. It was more like a weight had been lifted and I could focus on baseball again. Except I couldn't play.

In the third week I stared going to practices. Coach Harris and Wash had called together to tell me they wanted me to hang with the team while I was mending. And it was great. Guys kept coming up to me that first day to say, "Hey, we missed you." No one said anything about spots or my dumb move in LA, even though I would have been an easy target.

The second practice I went to, Coach came over and said, "Someone wants to meet you." It was the white-haired guy who came to watch us sometimes. Today I noticed the Oakleys and the Rolex.

"Well, Danny Manuel," he said without smiling. "The face of Ocelot."

"Not any more, Mr. Mancini."

"Well, you're better off."

I nodded.

"Look, it's a good lesson to learn while you're young. Choose your friends carefully. Choose people you can trust."

"Mr. Mancini—"

"Call me Pop."

"Pop, I'm sorry. Coach Washington said you wouldn't like the Ocelot thing, but I was thinking just about me . . . I just . . ." I felt like such a jerk. Pop was obviously a straight shooter, but somehow I'd been seduced by Ocelot. Strauss had dropped me the minute I was out of commission.

"Don't worry about it, Danny. And you did give us some thrills this year. I've seen a lot of baseball, and you've got talent. Talent and something else. Sometimes you almost seem to see what's happening before the ball's in play."

"Except for that one time," I said. That tickled Mancini. He laughed hard for a few seconds.

"Anyway," he said finally, "stop into my store sometime. I might have some work for you. That spotted stuff is making me a small fortune."

. . .

Meeting Pop was cool, but the best thing about those practices? It was hanging with Wash. I learned more about baseball in those four weeks than I had in the seventeen years before. All that time I'd been working on my physical skills, trying to show my talent. But Wash showed me that, as far as the *game* goes, I was still a rookie.

Wash taught me about pitching—what pitches worked in certain situations. He showed me what Coach was thinking when he positioned the fielders and where to hit the ball when there were guys on base with outs to spend. He was full of sayings. One of his favorites was, "The best is the enemy of the good."

"Like your famous catch," he explained. "That was the best. But going for it was not a good idea from a game standpoint. You usually try for a play you are confident you can execute and get acceptable results. Don't count on miracles; they don't happen often enough."

By week five I was traveling with the team to games. They let me warm up, but I wasn't allowed to run hard or even slide, and I wasn't allowed in the batting cage. Still, it felt good to wear the uniform again. By now I'd figured out that when my six weeks were up, we'd have only one tournament left. It would be right here in Vegas—a weeklong playoff among the six best teams in our association. It was our World Series.

My six-week injury suspension ended four days before the tournament started. The doctor cleared me to take batting practice and run a little, but no sliding.

"With your power," Nellie joked. "Why slide anyway?" I laughed. We both knew my "power" was nowhere near Nellie's.

I was talking to Darius pretty regularly now. I did know some things about fielding center, and he seemed grateful for advice. At one point I actually asked him about Kayla, who had stopped calling or writing me after that last email.

"We're history," Darius said. "That girl was just a jersey chaser, you know? Not really into me. Last I heard she was seeing some DJ in LA."

When the tournament started, even though I was theoretically cleared to play, I wasn't in the starting lineup. Coach was honest with me.

"Danny," he said, "you have a future in this game if you want it. I know to someone your age, it seems like now is all there is. But I'm not going to risk your future by playing you before you're really healthy." Then he winked at me. "Unless it's the only way we can win."

CHAPTER 19

As the tournament unfolded, it didn't look like my services would be needed. Frankly, we cruised. Our hitters were hitting. Our pitchers were pitching. We were the team we really could be. (Without me, I couldn't help but notice.)

Wash, sitting next to me on the bench, said at one point, "You know, you coach so guys can play like this. But when they do, you feel kind of unnecessary." By the weekend we knew we'd have a shot at the championship. Standing in our way were our old rivals, the Desert Eagles of Phoenix.

On Saturday, we kicked Eagle butt—or tail. Darius was the star, along with Carson. While our pitcher scattered six hits—one run scored on an error—Darius drove in three runs, stole two bases, and reached base on every at bat. That's just the way the week had gone for us. We beat the Eagles 6–1.

Sunday afternoon we were just as good, but we weren't lucky. Jonas pitched well, but every time an Eagle made contact with the ball it went someplace our fielders weren't. I heard some language from Wash that was new to me.

In the bottom of the ninth we were down one run. With two outs, we had a guy on second and Darius at the plate. Darius was hot this week, so we liked our chances, and sure enough, he absolutely ripped a line drive to left. Well, almost to left. The Eagle shortstop made a twisting leap and somehow came down with the ball in his glove. Game over.

All week I'd been in the dugout, keeping score. I thought just maybe Coach would start me in the last game, but no such luck. During the break Coach didn't say much, and he really didn't need to. We knew the Eagles; we just had to execute.

Which we did. At first. Darius walked and stole second. That was becoming like a stock play. We knew he had to be setting some kind of record for steals. Gus flew to right, and Darius made it to third on the sacrifice. Nellie singled him in before Sammy grounded into a double play.

Carson was pitching, of course. I suppose I could say something more about that; sometimes you heard grumbles about his dad's influence and all. But he really was our best pitcher, and tonight he looked it. Nobody touched him until the third inning, but their number-eight hitter touched him roughly then, clearing the fence by a good twenty yards.

The bottom of the third looked good for us. We had two on with no one out. Then Gus fanned, and Nellie hit into a double play.

Sammy's leadoff homer in the fourth inning put us ahead, but suddenly our hitters seemed to go to sleep. Of the next seven hitters, four struck out, one walked, and the rest grounded or popped up to the infield. Fortunately, the Eagles weren't taking advantage. Carson kept them scoreless through the same stretch.

Sammy doubled in the eighth, and Trip walked. Trip got doubled off by the next hitter. But Zack tripled, and the Runners went into the ninth with a 3–1 lead.

The first Eagles hitter in the ninth hit a screamer to center, over Darius's head. Darius started back but suddenly grabbed his leg and crumpled to the ground. Sammy streaked to the ball and managed to get it back in, but the Eagles hitter was standing on third base.

Coach, trainers, and the rest of the team on the field ran to Darius, who was rocking in pain, holding his right leg. Everyone hoped it was a cramp, but no one could know at this point. A hamstring? A knee? It was pretty clear Darius couldn't continue. After about five minutes Nellie and Sammy supported Darius as he hopped off the field.

Coach looked up and down the bench and finally said, "Danny, you're in. No rough stuff, understood?"

CHAPTER 20

I maybe should have been thinking, *Yeah! This is my big chance!* But I wasn't. The thing in the front of my mind was simply *Don't screw up!* That's what injuries do. They sow doubt where it wasn't growing before.

I had a job to do, though, and sure enough the next batter hit a fly to deep center. It wasn't the kind of ball I'd ever worried about before. It was high in the air, not far enough to leave the park, but I was almost shaking as I tried to let instinct take over and *just get it.*

And I did. The Eagles' base runner went home, of course. The crowd yelled, and I thought, *Wow, the Eagles have a lot of fans for an away game.* But the cheering kept up after he was in the dugout. I looked around and finally realized that it was me they were cheering for. Some of them were waving spotted towels, and I could hear people yelling my name and chanting, "Danny's back!"

It actually choked me up a little. I just felt grateful—for health, for the fun of baseball.

Coach decided they were getting after Carson, so he put Shotaro on the mound. Nick came out to talk with him, but he was nervous and let one pitch to the next batter get out over the plate, high and juicy. The batter, a lefty, jumped on it. We thought he'd pulled it foul, but the ump said it was inside the pole. Coach jumped out of the dugout and started yelling, waving his arms toward the seats on the foul side of right. But he knew better than anyone else that the demonstration wasn't going to do any good. The game was tied.

Shotaro walked the next guy, but the batter after him grounded to Trip for an easy double play. Coming up in the bottom of the ninth: Nick, Shotaro, and me.

Nick tripled. Our bench went crazy. There it was, the winning run sitting on third, no one out. Shotaro popped to second, though. It was my turn.

I hadn't batted in a game in almost two months. I took a really awkward cut at the first pitch and missed it ugly. Pitch two was high, and pitch three was inside. With a 2–1 count, I was sitting on a fastball. What I got, and what I missed, was a changeup.

"Calm down, Danny," I told myself. "The pitcher is just as nervous as you are." Which probably wasn't true, but he threw the next pitch low.

I tried to think about the situation from the pitcher's point of view. Wash had taught me. Risk/reward. A hit from me ended the game. If I wound up on first without hitting, they were still alive. I didn't expect a strike.

Ball four was outside. I took first base with one out and hoped Gus would do something.

He took a huge cut at the first pitch and missed. Same with the second. He looked totally juiced to save the game with a homer. Not a good thing. The third pitch was a ball, but on the next offering Gus hit a sharp grounder to the third baseman.

The third baseman should have gone to the plate. Nick was on his way. But the infielder instead chose the best over the good. He saw a double-play opportunity. I was headed for second with a good jump. I was out, but my job was to disrupt the double play.

I slid hard into second and into the second baseman, who was trying to turn the play as he got out of my way. I think it was his knee that hit the side of my head, but suddenly I heard the crowd yelling.

Gus was safe at first. The throw from second was wide. We had won.

The Eagles' coach ran out screaming about interference, but the play was clean—everyone saw it later thanks to the Ocelot cameras on site. We were the champions.

The first person to reach me—I was still on the ground at second—was Coach.

"Darn it, Danny, I said no rough stuff! Are you all right?"

Thankfully I was. I didn't feel any different than I would have before the concussion on that kind of play.

Nellie and Wash were the next people to get there, but I was getting up by then. The team swarmed out on the field, and the next thing I knew they were carrying me off. Just like after The Catch, only better.

ABOUT THE AUTHOR

Rick Jasper is a former middle school teacher and a long-time magazine editor and writer. A native of Kansas City, Missouri, he currently lives in Raleigh, North Carolina with his daughter.

"The road to the pros
starts here."

THE CATCH

When Danny makes "the catch," everyone seems interested in him. Girls text him, kids ask for autographs, and his highlight play even makes it on SportsCenter's Top Plays. A sports-gear executive tempts Danny with a big-money offer, and he decides to take advantage of his newfound fame. Danny agrees to wear the company's gear when he plays. But as his bank account gets bigger, so does his ego. Will Danny be able to keep his head in the game?

POWER HITTER

Sammy Perez has to make it to the big leagues. After his teammate's career-ending injury, the Roadrunners decided to play in a wood bat tournament to protect their pitchers. And while Sammy used to be a hotheaded, hard-hitting, home-run machine, he's now stuck in the slump of his life. Sammy thinks the wood bats are causing the problem, but his dad suggests that maybe he's not strong enough. Is Sammy willing to break the law and sacrifice his health to get an edge by taking performance-enhancing drugs? Can Sammy break out of his slump in time to get noticed by major-league scouts?

FORCED OUT

Zack Waddell's baseball IQ makes him one of the Roadrunners' most important players. When a new kid, Dustin, immediately takes their starting catcher's spot, Zack is puzzled. Dustin doesn't have the skills to be a starter. So Zack offers to help him with his swing in Dustin's swanky personal batting cages.

Zack accidentally overhears a conversation and figures out why Dustin is starting—and why the team is suddenly able to afford an expensive trip to a New York tournament. Will Zack's baseball instincts transfer off the field? Will the Roadrunners be able to stay focused when their team chemistry faces its greatest challenge yet?

THE PROSPECT

Nick Cosimo eats, breathes, and lives baseball. He's a place-hitting catcher, with a cannon for an arm and a calculator for a brain. Thanks to his keen eye, Nick is able to pick apart his opponents, taking advantage of their weaknesses. His teammates and coaches rely on his good instincts between the white lines. But when Nick spots a scout in the stands, everything changes. Will Nick alter his game plan to impress the scout enough to get drafted? Or will Nick put the team before himself?

OUT OF CONTROL

Carlos "Trip" Costas is a fiery shortstop with many talents and passions. His father is Julio Costas—yes, *the* Julio Costas, the famous singer. Unfortunately, Julio is also famous for being loud, controlling, and sometimes violent with Trip. Julio dreams of seeing his son play in the majors, but that's not what Trip wants.

When Trip decides to take a break from baseball to focus on his own music, his father loses his temper. He threatens to stop donating money to the team. Will the Roadrunners survive losing their biggest financial backer and their star shortstop? Will Trip have the courage to follow his dreams and not his father's?

HIGH HEAT

Pitcher Seth Carter had Tommy John surgery on his elbow in hopes of being able to throw harder. Now his fastball cuts through batters like a 90 mph knife through butter. But one day, Seth's pitch gets away from him. The *clunk* of the ball on the batter's skull still haunts Seth in his sleep and on the field. His arm doesn't feel like part of his body anymore, and he goes from being the ace everybody wanted to the pitcher nobody trusts. With the biggest game of the year on the line, can Seth come through for the team?

SOUTHSIDE HIGH

ARE YOU A SURVIVOR?

check out all the books in the

SURVIVING SOUTH SIDE

collection.

Bad Deal

Fish hates having to take ADHD meds. They help him concentrate but also make him feel weird. So when a cute girl needs a boost to study for tests, Fish offers her one of his pills. Soon more kids want pills, and Fish likes the profits. To keep from running out, Fish finds a doctor who sells phony prescriptions. But suddenly the doctor is arrested. Fish realizes he needs to tell the truth. But will that cost him his friends?

Recruited

Kadeem is a star quarterback for Southside High. He is thrilled when college scouts seek him out. One recruiter even introduces him to a college cheerleader and gives him money to have a good time. But then officials start to investigate illegal recruiting. Will Kadeem decide to help their investigation, even though it means the end of the good times? What will it do to his chances of playing in college?

Benito Runs

Benito's father had been in Iraq for over a year. When he returns, Benito's family life is not the same. Dad suffers from PTSD—post-traumatic stress disorder—and yells constantly. Benito can't handle seeing his dad so crazy, so he decides to run away. Will Benny find a new life? Or will he learn how to deal with his dad—through good times and bad?

PLAN B

Lucy has her life planned: She'll graduate and join her boyfriend at college in Austin. She'll become a Spanish teacher, and of course they'll get married. So there's no reason to wait, right? They try to be careful, but Lucy gets pregnant. Lucy's plan is gone. How will she make the most difficult decision of her life?

BEATEN

Keah's a cheerleader and Ty's a football star, so they seem like the perfect couple. But when they have their first fight, Ty is beginning to scare Keah with his anger. Then after losing a game, Ty goes ballistic and hits Keah repeatedly. Ty is arrested for assault, but Keah still secretly meets up with Ty. How can Keah be with someone she's afraid of? What's worse—flinching every time your boyfriend gets angry or being alone?

Shattered Star

Cassie is the best singer at Southside and dreams of being famous. She skips school to try out for a national talent competition. But her hopes sink when she sees the line. Then a talent agent shows up, and Cassie is flattered to hear she has "the look" he wants. Soon she is lying and missing rehearsal to meet with him. And he's asking her for more each time. How far will Cassie go for her shot at fame?